Dear Parent:

Congratulations! Your child is taking the first steps on an exciting journey. The destination? Independent reading!

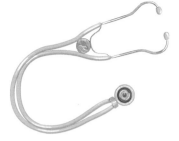

STEP INTO READING® will help your child get there. The program offers five steps to reading success. Each step includes fun stories and colorful art. There are also Step into Reading Sticker Books, Step into Reading Math Readers, Step into Reading Phonics Readers, Step into Reading Write-In Readers, and Step into Reading Phonics Boxed Sets—a complete literacy program with something for every child.

Learning to Read, Step by Step!

Ready to Read   Preschool–Kindergarten
• big type and easy words • rhyme and rhythm • picture clues
For children who know the alphabet and are eager to begin reading.

Reading with Help   Preschool–Grade 1
• basic vocabulary • short sentences • simple stories
For children who recognize familiar words and sound out new words with help.

Reading on Your Own   Grades 1–3
• engaging characters • easy-to-follow plots • popular topics
For children who are ready to read on their own.

Reading Paragraphs   Grades 2–3
• challenging vocabulary • short paragraphs • exciting stories
For newly independent readers who read simple sentences with confidence.

Ready for Chapters   Grades 2–4
• chapters • longer paragraphs • full-color art
For children who want to take the plunge into chapter books but still like colorful pictures.

STEP INTO READING® is designed to give every child a successful reading experience. The grade levels are only guides. Children can progress through the steps at their own speed, developing confidence in their reading, no matter what their grade.

Remember, a lifetime love of reading starts with a single step!

Visit us on the Web!
StepIntoReading.com
randomhouse.com/kids
www.barbie.com

Educators and librarians, for a variety of teaching tools, visit us at RHTeachersLibrarians.com

ISBN: 978-0-307-98112-7 (trade) — ISBN: 978-0-307-98114-1 (lib. bdg.)

Printed in the United States of America 10 9 8 7 6 5 4 3 2 1

STEP INTO READING®

STEP 2

Barbie™ i can be...

A Baby Doctor

Concept developed for Mattel by Egmont Creative Center

By Susan Marenco based on plots written by Giulia Conti

Adapted by Kristen L. Depken

Illustrated by Tino Santanach and Joaquin Canizares
with Pam Duarte

Random House 🏠 New York

Barbie wants
to be a baby doctor.
She goes
to the hospital.

She visits babies
in the nursery.
She will learn
to take care of them!

Barbie meets
Doctor Green.

She is a baby doctor.

Barbie meets
Nurse Kay.
She is a baby nurse.
They will teach Barbie
to take care of babies.

Barbie holds
a baby boy.

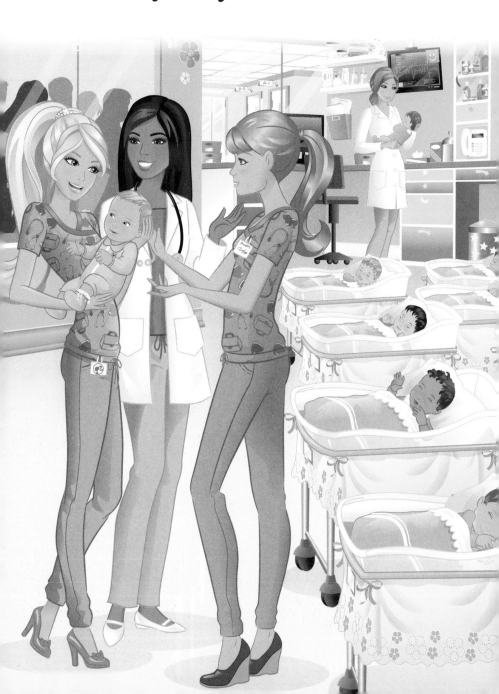

He starts to cry!

Barbie rocks
the baby.
He cries and cries.

Nurse Kay says
the baby is hungry.
She gets a bottle.

Barbie feeds the baby.

He stops crying!

The baby is done eating.
Nurse Kay shows Barbie
how to burp him.

Barbie puts the baby
on her shoulder.
She pats his back.
He burps!

Barbie smells
something funny.
The baby has
a dirty diaper.

Barbie changes
the baby's diaper.

Later she
gives him a bath.

It is time to play!
Barbie puts
the babies
on a mat.

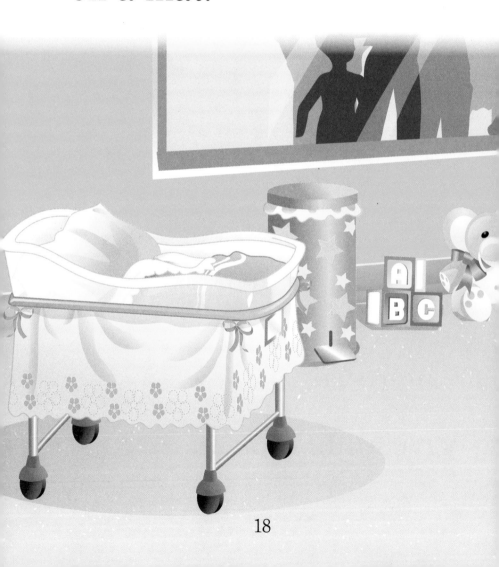

She shows them
a toy.
The babies love it!

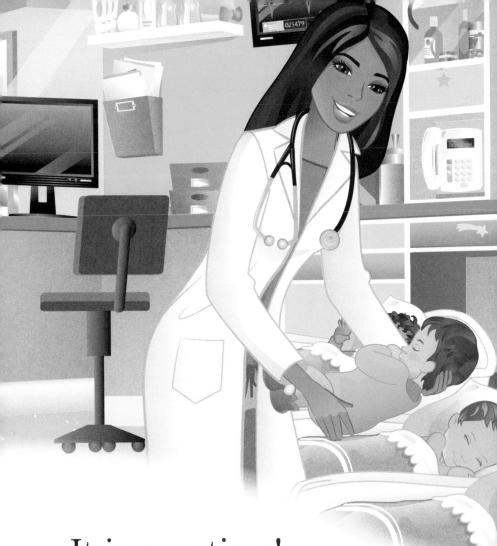

It is nap time!
Barbie and Doctor Green
put the babies
in their cribs.

They cover the babies
with blankets.

Soon all the babies
are asleep.

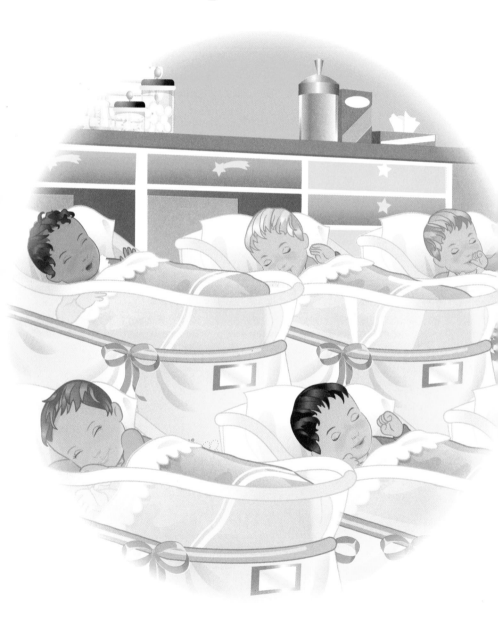

Another doctor comes
to the nursery.
He asks Barbie
and Nurse Kay
for help.

Barbie and Nurse Kay
meet a new baby girl.

They will take care
of the baby
while her mom rests.

Nurse Kay shows Barbie
how to hold
the new baby.
She is so tiny!

Barbie gives the baby
her first bath.

Barbie dresses the baby.

Then Barbie
brings the baby
to her mom.
The mom
will feed the baby.

Barbie shows the mom
how to burp the baby.
Doctor Green checks
on them.
Barbie does a great job!

The baby's
mom and dad
thank Barbie.

One day,
Barbie will be
a great baby doctor!